Izzy's Butterfly Garden

Written by Mary Roulston

Illustrated by Kelly O'Neill

Collins

Who and what is in this story?

Listen and say

Chen

Izzy

Snowy the rabbit

Download the audio at www.collins.co.uk/839692

William

Bib the cat

Faisal

Floss the dog

🎧 Izzy has got a garden. There are lots of flowers in the garden. It's very beautiful.

Izzy loves her garden. Izzy wants
a pet. Pets like gardens, too.

5

She doesn't know what pet to get.

All of her friends have got pets.

Chen and her dog visit Izzy's garden.

Chen says, "This is my dog.
She's called Floss.
Do you like dogs, Izzy?"

Izzy says, "Yes, I do. Hello, Floss!"

Izzy says, "Oh, no. My flowers!"

Chen says, "Come here, Floss!
Sorry, Izzy!"

Izzy says, "It's OK."

William and his cat visit Izzy's garden.

William says, "This is my cat.
He's called Bib. Do you like cats, Izzy?"

Izzy says, "Yes, I do. Hello, Bib!"

Izzy says, "Oh, no. My butterflies!"

William says, "Stop it, Bib! Sorry, Izzy!"
Izzy says, "It's OK."

Faisal and his rabbit visit Izzy's garden.

Faisal says, "This is my rabbit.
She's called Snowy.
Do you like rabbits, Izzy?"

Izzy says, "Yes, I do. Hello, Snowy."

Izzy says, "Oh, no. My flowers *and* my butterflies!"

Faisal says, "Stop eating, Snowy!
Sorry, Izzy!"

Izzy says, "It's OK."

Izzy thinks, "I like dogs, cats and rabbits, but I *love* my garden ...

... and my butterflies!"

Picture dictionary

Listen and repeat

butterfly

cat

dog

flower

garden

rabbit

1 Look and order the story

2 Listen and say

Collins

Published by Collins
An imprint of HarperCollins*Publishers*
Westerhill Road
Bishopbriggs
Glasgow
G64 2QT

HarperCollins*Publishers*
1st Floor, Watermarque Building
Ringsend Road
Dublin 4
Ireland

William Collins' dream of knowledge for all began with the publication of his first book in 1819.

A self-educated mill worker, he not only enriched millions of lives, but also founded a flourishing publishing house. Today, staying true to this spirit, Collins books are packed with inspiration, innovation and practical expertise. They place you at the centre of a world of possibility and give you exactly what you need to explore it.

© HarperCollins*Publishers* Limited 2020

10 9 8 7 6 5 4 3 2

ISBN 978-0-00-839692-3

www.collins.co.uk/elt

British Library Cataloguing in Publication Data

A catalogue record for this publication is available from the British Library.

Author: Mary Roulston
Illustrator: Kelly O'Neill (Beehive)
Series editor: Rebecca Adlard
Publishing manager: Lisa Todd
Product managers: Jennifer Hall and Caroline Green
In-house editor: Alma Puts Keren
Project manager: Emily Hooton
Editor: Rebecca Adlard
Proofreaders: Natalie Murray and Michael Lamb
Cover designer: Kevin Robbins
Typesetter: 2Hoots Publishing Services Ltd
Audio produced by id audio, London
Reading guide author: Katie Foufouti
Production controller: Rachel Weaver
Printed and bound by: GPS Group, Slovenia

MIX
Paper from
responsible sources
FSC™ C007454

Download the audio for this book and a reading guide for parents and teachers at www.collins.co.uk/839692